The Berenstain Bears
GET IN A FIGHT

When two small bears
Don't get along,
The grownups worry—
What went wrong?

A FIRST TIME BOOK®

The Berenstain Bears

GET IN A FIGHT

Stan & Jan
Berenstain

Random House 🏠 New York

Copyright © 1982 by Berenstains, Inc. All rights reserved under International and Pan-American Copyright Conventions. Published in the United States by Random House, Inc., New York, and simultaneously in Canada by Random House of Canada Limited, Toronto. *Library of Congress Cataloging in Publication Data:* Berenstain, Stan, 1923– . The Berenstain bears get in a fight. (Berenstain bears first time books) SUMMARY: After causing a family commotion when they fight with each other, the Berenstain cubs learn that sometimes even the best of friends don't get along. [1. Behavior—Fiction. 2. Bears—Fiction. 3. Brothers and sisters—Fiction. 4. Friendship—Fiction] I. Berenstain, Jan, 1923– . II. Title. III. Series: Berenstain, Stan, 1923– Berenstain bears first time books. PZ7.B4483Beo [E] 81-15866 AACR2 ISBN: 0-394-85132-3 (trade); 0-394-95132-8 (lib. bdg.) Manufactured in the United States of America 16 17 18 19 20

Most mornings, in Bear Country, the sun
rose to greet the day and the mockingbird
sang its copycat songs outside an upstairs
window of the bears' tree house.

And inside the tree house Brother
Bear and Sister Bear would wake up.

Brother and Sister usually got along very well.

They took turns nicely with the bathroom.

They said "please" and "thank you" at breakfast.

They often sat together on the school bus.

And after school they worked together happily on their special project—their own backyard tree house.

But one gray morning Brother and Sister didn't get along well at all! Maybe it was the weather—or maybe it was because the mockingbird slept late. But whatever it was, Brother and Sister Bear got into a big fight. . . .

Sister Bear opened her eyes and stretched. Then she sat up and let her legs dangle over the edge of her bed—right in Brother Bear's face. She didn't do it to be rude. It was just one of those things that happens with bunk beds.

But that morning Brother was not in a very good mood.

"Sister!" he shouted. "Get your dopey feet out of my face!"

"My feet aren't dopey, and they're not
in your face!" she shouted back.
"Get your dopey *face* out of my face!"
snarled Brother.

"You shut up!" snapped Sister . . .

and before Brother could answer,
she skipped into the
bathroom ahead of him.

She took a *very long time* . . .

brushing her teeth,

washing up,

and brushing her fur.

"You'd better come out of that
bathroom!" shouted Brother,
banging on the door.

"Brother Bear," said Papa, coming out of his bedroom, "you know better than to shout at your sister." "But she's taking too long in the bathroom," complained Brother, "and she's doing it on purpose!"

When Brother raised his fist
to bang on the door again, it opened
and out came Sister, all spruced up.
"Good morning, Papa,"
she said, as nice
as you please.
"Gr-r-r!"
said Brother.

Brother and Sister didn't say "please" and "thank you" that morning at breakfast— because they weren't speaking to each other.

And they didn't sit together on the school bus. Sister sat in the front and Brother sat way in the back.

That afternoon they made a line down the middle of their backyard tree house to show which half was whose. It wasn't much fun sitting up there in their tree house not speaking.

Especially when it began to rain—hard!

Later they kept on being mean by taking back the things they usually shared.

Sister took back her modeling clay—which Brother had made into dinosaurs—and rolled it into one big lump.

Brother took back his trucks and planes and put them on the top shelf where Sister couldn't reach them.

They got so angry that they forgot they weren't speaking and began shouting at each other even louder than before. Then Papa lost his temper and began shouting at them to stop shouting.

The neighbors didn't know which was worse—the big storm or the racket coming from the bears' house.

Mama had quite enough. She put two fingers to her mouth and whistled—*very very loudly*. Papa and the cubs were so surprised that they stopped shouting.

"I didn't know you could whistle like that, Mama," said Sister.

TWE-E-ET

"Well, I can. And I can also tell you," said Mama sternly, "that I've had quite enough of this foolish fighting. Why, I doubt you two even remember what you're fighting about!"

The cubs tried to remember, but they couldn't.

Mama took the cubs into her lap.
"Everybody gets into an argument
once in a while," she said. "Even
folks who love each
other very much."

"You and I don't have arguments," said Papa.

"Oh, yes, we do," said Mama.

"No, we don't," argued Papa.

"We're having one right now," said Mama, "about whether or not we have arguments!"

While Papa thought that one over, Mama went on to say that occasional arguments are part of living together.

"We get angry, even call each other names and say things we really don't mean—and after a while it's over."

"Like the storm?" asked Sister. The rain had almost stopped, and the sun was beginning to shine through the clouds.

"Yes," said Mama. "Like the storm."
"Look!" said Papa.

The sun shining on the last of
the rain had made a rainbow.

"A rainbow is something very beautiful that happens after a storm," said Mama, looking at the cubs.

"You mean like making up after a big fight?"

"Sort of," said Mama.

So Brother and Sister Bear
hugged and made up.
And got along just beautifully—
until the next time, anyway.

The Berenstain Bears
GET THE GIMMIES

When a cub's behavior
takes a turn for the worst,
it's hard for parents
to know what to do first.

A First Time Book®

The Berenstain Bears GET THE GIMMIES

Stan & Jan Berenstain

Random House 🏠 New York

Library of Congress Cataloging-in-Publication Data:
Berenstain, Stan. The Berenstain bears get the gimmies. (A First time book)
SUMMARY: Gran and Gramps come up with a plan to help selfish Brother and Sister Bear get rid of a bad case of the galloping greedy gimmies. [1. Selfishness—Fiction. 2. Behavior—Fiction. 3. Bears—Fiction] I. Berenstain, Jan. II. Title. III. Series: Berenstain, Stan. First time books. PZ7.B4483Beoh 1988 [E] 88-42587 ISBN: 0-394-80566-6 (pbk.); 0-394-90566-0 (lib. bdg.)

Manufactured in the United States of America 2 3 4 5 6 7 8 9 0

Of course, the members of the Bear family, who lived in the big tree house down a sunny dirt road in Bear Country, loved each other. They loved each other very much. Brother and Sister Bear loved their mama and papa. Naturally, Mama and Papa Bear loved their cubs, and, of course, they were nice to them— as nice as they could be.

But sometimes, *sometimes* they were a little too nice. Sometimes the cubs got too many treats, too many toys, and too many rides on the Bucking Duck at the mall.

Maybe that's why Brother and Sister Bear got the gimmies. Or maybe it was because there were treats, toys, and fun things to do wherever they looked—at the supermarket, at the mall, on TV, and just about every which-where.

Maybe that was why they began making a fuss to get what they wanted—especially at the supermarket checkout, where there were always stacks and stacks of candy and other goodies.

"Now, cubs," Mama Bear said as the family got into the checkout line and she saw that old gimmie gleam in their eyes, "we can't have a big fuss every time we pass candy. I simply won't stand for it."

"But, Mama," whined Sister. "They have Gummy Gumballs! My favorite!"

"And Chewy Chompers! *My* favorite!" whined Brother.

"Now, hush!" said Mama. "I simply won't listen to another word..."

That's when Papa Bear smiled and said, "Now, Mama, you're only young once," and handed the cubs their favorite treats.

"It's only too true," said Mama as they were
leaving the supermarket, "that you're only young
once. But that's all the more reason to learn
proper behavior while you're still young, and I
certainly think—"

"Look! Look!" shouted Sister. "A new ride!"

"Hey, a Bucking Frog!" shouted Brother. "That
looks even better than the Bucking Duck! May we
ride it, please? May we? May we? Please!"

Now, Papa had just bought them treats, and he thought that was enough for one day. But the cubs made such a fuss that he sighed, dug into his pocket, and put some money in the slot.

Papa looked at Mama and shrugged. "Cubs will be cubs," he said.

"It may be true that cubs will be cubs," said Mama as they walked across the parking lot to their car. "But that's no excuse for jumping up and down and making a scene every time they see something they want—"

"Look! Look!" shouted the cubs once again. "Little rubber cats that stick out their tongues when you squeeze them!"

"Cubs," said Mama, "that will be quite enough! I don't want to hear another word..."

"Oh please!" they shouted. "May we have them? Please! Please! Please!" Papa decided it was time to put a stop to all the fussing.

"Stop that fussing!" he said in his loudest Papa Bear voice. But they were making such a commotion they didn't even hear him. Sister was jumping up and down so hard that she fell over backward and started kicking her feet in the air.

"Please! Please!" shouted the cubs so loudly that the whole parking lot took notice.

"Er—" said embarrassed Papa to the toy seller, "two of those rubber pussycats, please."

The rubber pussycats not
only stuck out their tongues
when you squeezed them, they
went squeak-squeak as well.
And they squeak-squeaked
all the way home.

Mama was quite annoyed by the time they got back to the tree house, but Papa was so angry he could hardly speak. It wasn't until the cubs had gone about their business and Mama had made a pot of tea that Papa's voice came back loud and clear.

"Of all the outrageous, disgraceful, *embarrassing* behavior I have ever seen," he roared, "that selfish, greedy performance by our cubs was the worst! Brother and Sister have the worst case of the galloping greedy gimmies I've ever seen!"

"Yes," said Mama, calmly sipping her tea. "But have you ever stopped to think about *why* they have the gimmies? Perhaps their greedy behavior isn't all their fault. Perhaps it's partly our fault for giving in every time they make a fuss."

Papa listened quietly. "Perhaps so," he said.

"It's up to us," she continued, "to explain things to them—to help them understand why it's important not to be greedy."

Then Papa called the cubs in for a talking-to. He told them why it wasn't a good idea to be selfish and greedy and want everything in sight.

"Selfish, greedy cubs," he explained, "can never be happy, because you just can't have everything you want all the time—life isn't like that. Do you understand?"

"Oh yes, Papa. We understand," they said.

He talked to them about "counting their blessings," which meant enjoying the things they had instead of forever wanting more and more and more.

"Does that make sense to you?" he asked.

"Oh yes, Papa," they said. "It makes a lot of sense."

That's when the cubs heard the sound of a familiar car door. It was Grizzly Gramps and Gran come to call.

Brother and Sister ran to open the front door, and as Gramps and Gran came up the steps, they made the biggest fuss yet.

"Whaja-bringme?" they screamed. "Whaja-bringme? Whaja-bringme?!" That did it.

"Up to your room!" roared Papa. "Up to your room and no TV or treats for a week! For a *month*! For a *year*!"

The cubs knew this wasn't the time to argue. They scurried up the stairs and into their room.

"We seem to have come at a bad time!" said Gran.

"What about these things we brought with us?" asked Gramps. "A puzzle for Brother and a top for Sister?"

"Your presents will have to wait, Gramps," answered Mama. "I'm afraid Brother and Sister have a bad case of the gimmies."

"The *galloping greedy* gimmies," added Papa. "The worst case I've ever seen."

The cubs opened their door a crack to listen.

"The worst case, ya say?" said Gramps, looking Papa in the eye. "Seems to me you were quite a gimmie-cub yourself when you were little."

Brother and Sister sneaked to the top of the stairs so they could hear better.

"I was?" said Papa.

RUFE GRIZZLY'S GENERAL STORE

"Of course, we didn't have malls or supermarkets back then. But there was old Rufe Grizzly's General Store. Wonderful place. Sold just about everything—honey cake, licorice sticks, molasses apples, and all sorts of toys and novelties. And did you ever have the gimmies! Did you ever! You wanted everything in sight. Downright embarrassing. Why, it got so bad we couldn't go there anymore."

"So we worked out a deal," said Gran. "When it came time for a trip to the General Store, we had you decide on a treat ahead of time. It could be a sweet, a toy, or a book—and that was it for the day."

"Right," said Gramps. "And if you came down with the gimmies, we went right home and you got *nothing*!"

"That sounds like a pretty good plan to me," said Mama.

"Me too," said Papa.

The cubs tiptoed back to their room. It sounded okay to them, too.

The next time the Bear family went to the supermarket, they tried the Gramps-and-Gran plan. And it worked!

Brother decided he would get a book about dinosaurs, and Sister wanted a new box of crayons.

Mama and Papa were very proud when the cubs passed the candy rack without so much as a peep. Brother and Sister were pretty proud of themselves, too.

But then they heard it: the familiar sound of a cub with a bad case of the gimmies. The kicking, screaming cub was just behind them in the checkout line. You never *heard* such a fuss.

"What outrageous, disgraceful, embarrassing behavior!" said Sister. *"May we leave?"*

"Yeah," said Brother. "Let's get out of here."

And that's how Brother and Sister
Bear got rid of a pretty bad case
of the galloping greedy gimmies.